# Space Cadet Legacy

in

# "Green Across the Board"

Book #37 in the Space Cadet Richard Series

Russell Vance McFall

---

**Published by Ordained Path Books**
For permissions or inquiries:
ordainedpathbooks@gmail.com

---

Cover illustration and interior artwork generated by AI under the direction of the author.

**First Edition**

---

"Your word is a lamp to my feet
And a light to my path."
—Psalm 119:105 (NASB)

---

Ordained Path Books is dedicated to stories that reflect timeless truths, courage, and the quiet strength of faith—guided by purpose and written to inspire the next generation.

---

**ISBN (Paperback):** 978-1-972724-03-3
**ISBN (Hardcover):**

---

Printed in the United States of America
**Version 1.0 — March 2026**

# Dedication

For those learning to carry responsibility—
one decision at a time.

## About the Emblem — Delta Directive

The Delta Emblem is not a symbol of authority.
It is a reminder of responsibility.

At its center is a triangle, representing the three virtues that make the Delta Directive possible:

**Integrity** — truth held even when unseen.
**Unity** — trust shared and protected within the team.
**Discretion** — restraint exercised without recognition.

Remove any one of these, and trust does not fail loudly.
It erodes quietly.

---

Beneath the triangle are four stars, representing the cadets entrusted with the Directive.

The stars are positioned below the triangle to remind them that character must rest on something greater than individual achievement—and that responsibility must come before recognition.

---

The emblem carries no weapons, no rank, and no symbols of force.

It does not grant authority.

It marks a commitment.

---

Delta is not about power.

It is about choosing what must be protected—
and carrying what must remain, even when no one is watching
and no credit is given.

---

And sometimes—

it is about knowing when not to carry something at all.

When responsibility belongs to another,
the greater act is not to take it—
but to return it, and trust it will be held.

---

Delta is not measured by what is done.

It is measured by what is rightly carried—
and what is rightly left in the hands of others.

## Cast of Characters

---

**Richard Taylor**

Commanding officer of the *Specter One*. Calm, disciplined, and attentive to context, Richard leads through restraint rather than control. He understands that not every problem is his to solve—and that leadership sometimes requires allowing others to carry responsibility, even when the outcome is uncertain.

---

**Ashton Quinn**

Operations and situational-awareness specialist. Ashton excels at recognizing patterns that emerge indirectly rather than through obvious signals. She senses when intervention would help—and when it would take something important away.

---

**Dooley Lewis**

Systems and engineering lead. Practical, precise, and deeply trusted, Dooley focuses on stability without overreach. He understands both the strength and the limits of automation—and respects the role of human judgment within it.

---

**Milo Santiago**

Timing and data-analysis specialist. Young but perceptive, Milo notices subtle shifts in behavior as easily as changes in data. His questions are simple—but often reach deeper than expected.

---

**Whizzy**

A small, spherical support AI with a single central eye and retractable limbs. Whizzy observes without urgency and notices fine structural detail others might miss. Rarely intrusive, Whizzy contributes with quiet precision when needed.

---

**Ship AI**

---

**Mother**

The advanced artificial intelligence aboard *Specter One.* Mother monitors, coordinates, and executes ship operations with high autonomy and minimal commentary. She does not speculate or interpret beyond defined parameters—and records each mission as operating within established tolerance.

---

**Settlement Leadership & Citizens**

---

**Elara Venn**

Senior Council Member. Calm, precise, and thoughtful, Elara carries the memory of the colony's founding crisis as a child. She believes in the system that followed—but understands, perhaps more than most, what it cost to build it.

---

**Tomas Hale**

Director of Operations & Safety Complex. Practical and steady, Tomas represents the generation that refined and trusted the optimization system. He values stability and has seen the system succeed—but is learning that stability and participation are not the same.

---

**Mira Solen**

Systems Liaison and Phase Two Planning Coordinator. Organized, warm, and optimistic, Mira grew up entirely within the optimized system. She serves as a bridge between the cadets and the settlement, helping others understand how things work—while beginning to notice what may be missing.

---

## The Maren Family

---

**Jonah Maren**

Habitat maintenance technician. Practical and dependable, Jonah trusts the system because it has consistently provided stability for his family.

---

**Lysa Maren**

Agricultural dome supervisor. Thoughtful and steady, Lysa understands both the system's value and the responsibility it carries for sustaining life on the plateau.

---

**Kira Maren**

Their daughter, age 11. Curious and observant, Kira has grown up entirely within the system's guidance. Her simple questions reveal assumptions others no longer notice.

---

## Institutions & Frameworks

---

**The Optimization Engine**

The central system governing environmental balance, resource allocation, and structural load across the settlement. Designed to prevent instability, it has become both a tool and a trusted authority.

---

**The Founding Stability Protocol**

The guiding framework developed after the early drought allocation failure. It prioritizes predictive modeling and minimizes human estimation during critical decisions—shaping both the system and the culture of the settlement.

---

**The Delta Directive**

A guiding authority shaping the cadets' actions. It emphasizes responsibility without recognition, authority without force, and restraint without explanation. It defines not what must be done—but what must be carried—and, at times, what must be returned.

# Contents

# Chapter 1 — Orders

The ship moved steadily through open space, its motion so smooth it was almost impossible to feel.

Inside, the low hum of the systems blended into the background—a constant, familiar presence that no one paid much attention to anymore. Light from the forward viewport stretched across the control deck in a soft, even glow, broken only by the occasional flicker of a passing navigation marker.

Richard stood near the forward console, reviewing a set of routine system reports. Nothing unusual. Power distribution stable. Environmental systems well within tolerance. The kind of quiet, predictable status that marked most days aboard.

Behind him, Milo sat at a side station, scrolling through a data stream with more interest than it probably deserved. Dooley leaned back slightly in his chair, one foot resting against the lower brace of the console, watching a diagnostic trace complete its cycle. Ashton stood near the viewport, her attention not on any single point, but on the pattern of movement beyond it.

No one was in a hurry.

The ship wasn't either.

A soft tone sounded—barely more than a shift in the background noise.

Richard glanced down as a new message appeared on the console.

He didn't say anything at first. He read it through once, then again, slower.

Dooley noticed the pause before anyone else.

"Something change?" he asked, not turning yet.

Richard didn't answer immediately. He reached forward, adjusted the display, and let the message expand into a clearer format.

"Assignment update," he said at last.

That was enough.

Milo turned in his chair. Ashton shifted her attention from the viewport. Dooley leaned forward, resting both feet on the floor again.

No one rushed. They simply gathered.

Richard stepped back slightly from the console so they could all see.

For a moment, there was only the quiet glow of the display between them.

Milo read faster than the others.

"Phase Two certification?" he said. "What's Phase Two?"

Dooley exhaled lightly through his nose, considering how to answer.

"It's not as complicated as it sounds," he said. "Think of a structure that's been holding steady under one set of conditions. Everything balanced. Everything predictable."

Milo nodded, waiting.

"Phase Two means changing those conditions," Dooley continued. "More load. More movement. You're not just holding things steady anymore—you're letting them flex a little. See how they carry it."

Milo tilted his head slightly. "So… you're making it less stable?"

Dooley shook his head. "Not less stable. Less controlled."

Ashton spoke then, her voice quiet but precise.

"Certification, not correction."

Milo glanced toward her. "Meaning?"

"We're not there to change how they operate," she said. "We're there to verify that what they've built can handle what comes next."

Richard watched them for a moment, then added, evenly:

"We verify capacity. That's it."

The words settled into the space between them.

No one argued. No one needed to.

Milo looked back at the display, reading more carefully now. Dooley leaned in slightly, already scanning the technical details. Ashton's gaze returned briefly to the viewport, as if placing the assignment into a wider context.

Routine had shifted—but only slightly.

Richard reached forward and confirmed the assignment.

A moment later, the navigation display adjusted. A new vector appeared, clean and direct.

The ship responded without hesitation, turning smoothly toward its next destination.

No announcement followed.

Just a quiet change in direction.

## Chapter 2 — The Plateau

The plateau came into view gradually.

At first it was only a shift in color—a muted green against the darker tones of the surrounding terrain. Then the edges sharpened, and the shape resolved into something more deliberate. A wide, elevated plain stretched outward beneath them, its surface broken by long lines of low vegetation that bent gently with the wind.

Beyond it, the land dropped away into uneven ridges and shadowed valleys.

But the plateau itself remained clean.

Intentional.

Richard stood at the forward viewport as the ship began its descent. From this height, the settlement revealed itself in quiet detail—structures arranged with careful spacing, each one positioned with a kind of measured balance that made the entire layout feel considered rather than grown.

At the center, the Operations & Safety Complex anchored everything. Its broad base and reinforced exterior stood out against the lighter structures around it. From there, the habitat districts spread outward in a loose ring, their shapes softened by green space and open pathways. Beyond them, two agricultural domes curved upward along the plateau's edges, their surfaces catching the light in a faint, muted sheen.

Farther out still, he could see the outlines of additional structures—complete, but inactive.

Expansion districts.

Waiting.

Behind him, Dooley stepped closer, leaning slightly to get a better angle.

"Well," he said quietly, "they like things even."

Milo moved up beside him, eyes scanning across the layout.

"It doesn't look crowded," he said.

"It's not," Ashton replied. "Everything has space."

Richard didn't comment. He watched the central complex for a moment longer, then shifted his attention to the approach markers appearing along the plateau surface.

They were already active.

Thin lines of light traced a landing path across the ground, adjusting subtly as the ship descended. The alignment shifted in small increments—barely noticeable unless you were looking for it—keeping the approach vector centered with quiet precision.

"They're tracking us early," Dooley noted.

"Or expecting you," Ashton said.

The ship continued downward, responding smoothly as the guidance path refined itself beneath them.

No turbulence.

No correction.

Just a steady, uninterrupted descent.

The landing zone came into full view near the center of the settlement—a broad, open space bordered by low structures and a series of evenly spaced light columns. As they approached, the lights adjusted again, narrowing slightly as if focusing their attention.

Milo noticed.

"They do that automatically?" he asked.

Dooley nodded once. "Looks like it."

The ship settled onto the surface with a soft, controlled contact. There was no jolt—just a gentle shift in weight as the landing struts absorbed the final motion.

For a moment, everything was still.

Then the systems around them powered down in sequence, the steady hum of flight giving way to a quieter, grounded silence.

Richard turned toward the exit.

"Let's go."

---

The air outside was cooler than he expected.

Not cold—just clean, with a faint dryness that carried easily on the wind. It moved steadily across the plateau, brushing through the low grass and catching against the edges of the nearby structures before continuing on without interruption.

There were no barriers to stop it.

No walls to break it.

Just open space.

Milo stepped down behind him, pausing briefly as he looked out across the settlement.

"It's… quiet," he said.

"It's controlled," Dooley replied.

Ashton didn't speak. She was watching the movement of the grass instead—the way it bent in unison, then settled, then shifted again.

Patterns.

Richard followed the path marked out from the landing area toward the central plaza. The ground beneath his feet was firm, but not rigid—designed to absorb stress without giving way. Even here, the structure was doing its work.

Waiting for them, just beyond the edge of the landing zone, stood a single figure.

She was already in position.

Not standing at attention—just present, as if she had been there long enough for the moment to feel natural.

As they approached, she stepped forward with an easy, practiced motion.

"Welcome to the plateau," she said, her tone warm but measured. "I'm Mira Solen. Systems liaison and Phase Two coordinator."

Richard inclined his head slightly. "Richard."

She acknowledged the others in turn, her gaze moving smoothly from one to the next.

"I've been assigned to assist during your certification," she continued. "If you need access to any district or system layer, I'll coordinate it."

Dooley glanced past her toward the central complex. "We'll probably start there."

Mira nodded. "That's expected."

There was a brief pause—not uncomfortable, just transitional.

Milo looked past her toward the outer edge of the settlement, where one of the agricultural domes rose against the horizon.

"You've got a lot of room out here," he said.

"We planned for growth," Mira replied.

She turned slightly, gesturing toward the structures around them.

"Everything you see is part of the Phase One configuration. Stable, balanced, predictable." She hesitated for a fraction of a second, her gaze shifting briefly toward a nearby display panel before returning to them.

"We learned to be careful."

The words were simple.

She didn't explain them.

Instead, she stepped aside, motioning them forward toward the heart of the settlement.

"If you're ready," she said, "we can begin with the central systems briefing."

Richard nodded once.

And together, they walked toward the Operations & Safety Complex, the wind moving steadily at their backs as the plateau stretched wide and open around them.

## Chapter 3 — The Briefing

The Operations & Safety Complex sat at the center of the settlement like an anchor.

Up close, its structure felt different from the surrounding buildings. The outer walls were thicker, reinforced in a way that made the entire structure appear grounded—less like something placed on the plateau and more like something built into it.

Mira led them toward a wide entryway set slightly below grade. As they approached, the doors opened without sound, revealing a corridor that extended inward with clean, uninterrupted lines.

"Core systems are housed below the main level," she said. "Most of the load distribution and environmental controls are managed from there."

Dooley gave a small nod, already studying the construction. "You kept the critical layers centralized."

"It simplifies coordination," Mira replied.

They moved inside.

The air shifted subtly—cooler, more controlled. The sound of the wind faded behind them, replaced by a quieter, more contained environment. Lighting along the corridor adjusted as they walked, brightening slightly ahead of them and dimming behind.

No one commented on it.

At the end of the corridor, the space opened into a broader chamber.

The central systems room was larger than the exterior suggested, its structure supported by evenly spaced columns that rose into a ceiling lined with recessed lighting. Between them, layered displays hovered in organized sections, each one presenting a different aspect of the settlement's operation.

Power distribution. Environmental balance. Structural load mapping.

Everything was active.

Everything was stable.

And everything was arranged so it could be understood at a glance.

Richard slowed slightly as they entered, taking in the layout.

"This is your primary control layer?" he asked.

"It is," Mira said. "All major systems route through here."

"You keep redundancy local or distributed?" Dooley asked.

"Both," she replied. "Primary control is centralized. Secondary responses are distributed across district nodes."

Dooley nodded once. "Balanced."

Mira stepped aside as they approached the central console.

Someone was already there.

She stood with her attention on one of the primary displays, reviewing a set of structural readings. At their approach, she turned—not quickly, not with surprise, but with the kind of awareness that suggested she had known they were there before they arrived.

"Elara Venn," Mira said. "Senior Council."

Elara inclined her head slightly.

"Welcome," she said.

Her voice was steady. Not formal, not informal—simply precise.

Richard returned the nod. "Richard."

She acknowledged the others in the same measured way, her gaze moving from one to the next without hesitation.

"We appreciate your timely arrival," she said. "Phase One stability has been maintained within acceptable margins. Expansion authorization is pending certification."

Her attention shifted briefly to the display beside her. The information adjusted slightly, reorganizing itself into a more focused set of data points.

She waited a fraction of a second—just long enough to confirm the change—then continued.

"Your assignment parameters have been transmitted, but I'll summarize."

She stepped closer to the central projection. A layered model of the settlement appeared between them, its structure rendered in clean, segmented detail.

"Phase Two introduces increased environmental tolerance and expanded population capacity," she said. "This will alter load distribution across all primary systems."

The model shifted, highlighting stress points in soft gradients of color.

"Your role is to verify that the existing structure can support those changes."

Dooley leaned in slightly, studying the projection. "Manual overrides are part of that?"

"They are," Elara said. "Override pathways must be accessible at all critical junctions prior to activation."

"Installed or verified?" Dooley asked.

"Installed where absent. Verified where present."

He nodded once. "Understood."

Elara's gaze moved briefly across the display again, then returned to them.

"Once certification is complete, Phase Two activation may proceed."

Milo shifted his weight slightly. "And if it's not?"

Elara answered without hesitation.

"Then it does not."

There was no emphasis in the words.

No pressure.

Just a clear boundary.

Ashton spoke next.

"This is a structural certification," she said. "Not a behavioral assessment."

Elara looked at her for a moment—just long enough to register the distinction.

"That is correct," she said.

Richard stepped forward slightly, his attention on the projection.

"We verify capacity," he said. "Nothing beyond that."

Elara held his gaze for a brief moment, then inclined her head once.

"Agreed."

There was a pause.

Not empty—just complete.

Then Elara reached toward the console and adjusted the display again, bringing up a more detailed structural map.

"Initial access has been granted to the primary system layers," she said. "Mira will coordinate any additional requirements."

She hesitated briefly, her attention resting on a set of projected tolerance ranges.

"When those tolerances are widened," she said, "how much variation is considered acceptable?"

The question was asked evenly.

Technical.

Precise.

Richard answered just as evenly.

"Within the margins defined by the system's design," he said. "No more."

Elara considered that for a moment, then nodded.

"Understood."

She stepped back slightly, clearing space at the console.

"You may begin at your discretion."

There was nothing more to add.

Dooley moved first, already bringing up a deeper system layer. Milo shifted to a secondary display, scanning through incoming data. Ashton remained where she was for a moment longer, her attention not on the numbers, but on the patterns between them.

Richard stayed at the center, watching the system as a whole.

Outside, the wind continued to move across the plateau.

Inside, everything remained steady.

For now.

## Chapter 4 — The Greeting Wall

---

The wind met them again as they stepped out of the Operations Complex.

Inside, the air had been still—controlled, contained. Out here, it moved freely across the plateau, brushing against the structures and slipping through the open spaces between them without resistance.

For a moment, no one spoke.

The shift was subtle, but noticeable.

Mira waited just outside the entryway, as if she had expected them to emerge at that exact moment.

"Before we continue," she said, "there's something you should see."

She turned and began walking toward the center of the settlement.

The path led them back toward the public plaza, where the landing zone opened into a broader space bordered by low structures and evenly spaced light columns. The ground here was smoother, designed for gathering rather than transit, with wide walkways that curved gently around a central feature.

From a distance, it didn't stand out.

Just another structure.

Clean. Balanced. In place.

But as they approached, its purpose became clearer.

A wall—broad and rectangular, its surface finished in the same muted tones as the surrounding buildings. No decoration. No markings beyond a single embedded display that stretched across its center.

It wasn't large enough to dominate the plaza.

But it was positioned so that no one entering the space could avoid seeing it.

Mira slowed slightly as they neared it.

"This is part of the original design," she said. "It's been here since early Phase One."

She didn't say anything more.

She didn't need to.

The display activated as they came within range.

The surface shifted from neutral to illuminated, the text appearing in clean, evenly spaced lines.

No animation.

No emphasis.

Just words.

---

**ALL CRITICAL DECISIONS ARE GUIDED BY OPTIMAL SYSTEM MODELING**
**VARIANCE IS REDUCED TO PRESERVE STABILITY**
**CONSISTENCY ENSURES SURVIVAL**

---

The wind moved across the plaza, brushing lightly against the wall before continuing on.

Milo read the lines once, then again.

"So… everything goes through the system?" he asked.

Mira nodded. "For critical functions, yes."

Dooley studied the display a moment longer, his expression thoughtful rather than concerned.

"It's efficient," he said.

"It is," Mira replied.

Ashton didn't speak. Her gaze remained on the wording, not the display itself, as if measuring the space between what was written and what was meant.

Richard stood still.

The message was simple.

Clear.

And complete.

No argument.

No explanation.

Just a statement of how things were done.

After a moment, the display dimmed slightly, returning to its neutral state as their presence registered as complete.

Mira turned, gesturing toward the rest of the settlement.

"There's more to cover," she said. "If you're ready."

No one answered immediately.

Then Richard nodded once.

They moved on.

Behind them, the wall remained where it had always been—quiet, steady, and unchanged—its message waiting for the next set of eyes that would pause long enough to read it.

## Chapter 5 — The System Beneath

The transition back into the Operations Complex was immediate.

The wind disappeared behind them as the doors closed, replaced once again by the quiet, controlled air of the interior. The sounds of the plateau—soft, constant, uncontained—gave way to something more precise.

Measured.

Contained.

Mira led them deeper this time, past the main systems chamber and into a narrower corridor that angled downward beneath the central structure.

"Sublevels handle most of the distribution work," she said. "Primary systems route through the upper layer, but load balancing and environmental control are managed below."

The lighting shifted as they descended, adjusting to a softer, more focused range. The walls were closer here, the structure more visible—reinforced supports running at regular intervals, embedded conduits tracing steady lines along the surfaces.

Everything felt closer to the work.

Dooley ran a hand lightly along one of the exposed structural panels as they passed.

"Good access design," he said. "You didn't hide anything important."

"It makes maintenance easier," Mira replied.

"And inspection," he added.

She inclined her head slightly. "That too."

At the base of the corridor, the space opened again—smaller than the main chamber above, but denser. Systems were arranged in tighter configurations here, with direct access points built into the surrounding structure.

Someone was already working.

He stood near a recessed console, one hand resting lightly against the edge as he reviewed a sequence of data moving across the display. His posture was relaxed, but attentive—someone used to being where things mattered.

"Tomas Hale," Mira said. "Director of Operations."

Tomas glanced up briefly, then stepped back from the console.

"Welcome," he said. "I was expecting you."

His tone was straightforward, without formality.

Richard nodded. "Richard."

Tomas acknowledged the others with a brief glance, then gestured toward the surrounding systems.

"Core distribution layers are here," he said. "You'll have access to the primary grid, environmental channels, and structural mapping nodes."

Dooley stepped forward, already looking past him at the nearest interface.

"You're running live balancing across all districts?" he asked.

"All active zones," Tomas replied. "Expansion districts are on minimal load."

Dooley nodded once. "Good."

He reached toward the console, bringing up a deeper layer of the system.

The display shifted, expanding into a more detailed map—lines of energy flow, structural load gradients, environmental pressure zones. Everything was in motion, but controlled, each element adjusting in response to the others with quiet precision.

Milo moved to a secondary panel, pulling up a stream of variance data. Ashton remained slightly behind them, her attention moving between the displays rather than focusing on any one.

Richard watched the system as a whole.

At first, it looked exactly as it should.

Balanced.

Responsive.

Stable.

Then Dooley leaned in slightly.

"Hold on," he said.

He adjusted the display, isolating a section of the structural grid near one of the agricultural domes.

For a brief moment, a spike appeared—small, but clear.

Then it disappeared.

Smoothed out almost immediately.

Milo frowned slightly, bringing up the same region on his panel.

"I saw that too," he said. "There was a variance spike."

Tomas stepped closer, glancing at the display.

"Normal fluctuation," he said. "The system compensates."

Dooley didn't disagree. He just watched the data a moment longer.

"Fast," he said.

"It's designed to be," Tomas replied.

Another spike appeared—different location this time. Smaller.

Again, it vanished almost as quickly as it formed.

Ashton stepped forward slightly.

"It's not just compensating," she said quietly. "It's smoothing the pattern."

Tomas looked at her, considering that.

"Yes," he said after a moment. "That's part of the design."

"To reduce visible instability?" she asked.

"To reduce instability," he said.

There was a slight difference.

He didn't press it.

Milo continued scanning the data, his brow furrowed in concentration.

"It's limiting the variance range," he said. "Anything outside a narrow band gets pulled back in."

"Within safe margins," Tomas added.

Dooley straightened slightly, folding his arms.

"You've been running like this the whole time?" he asked.

"Since the protocol update," Tomas said. "It keeps the system predictable."

Dooley gave a small nod.

"Predictable's good," he said.

Tomas allowed a faint hint of a smile.

"It has been."

There was no defensiveness in the statement.

Just confidence.

Richard stepped closer to the central display.

"Manual override access points?" he asked.

Tomas gestured toward a series of embedded panels along the far wall.

"Limited," he said. "Most of those haven't been used in years."

Dooley glanced in that direction.

"That's usually when you need them," he said.

Tomas didn't argue.

He just nodded once.

"Then it's good you're here."

The system continued its quiet work around them—adjusting, compensating, smoothing.

Everything held.

Everything stayed within bounds.

Richard watched the flow of data for a moment longer, then shifted his attention slightly—not to any one point, but to the way the system moved as a whole.

There was no strain visible.

No pressure.

Nothing unresolved.

And yet—

He didn't say it.

Not yet.

"Let's begin mapping the full load distribution," he said instead.

Dooley nodded, already moving.

Milo adjusted his display. Ashton stepped closer to the central grid.

Tomas returned to his position beside them, watching as they began.

Above them, the plateau stretched wide and open.

Below, the system held everything in place.

## Chapter 6 — What the System Covers

Time passed without announcement.

There was no clear marker for it—no shift in lighting or tone, no indication beyond the gradual familiarity that settled into the space as the cadets moved deeper into their work.

The systems around them continued their steady operation, each layer adjusting in response to the others with quiet precision. What had first appeared complex now felt structured. Understandable.

Predictable.

Dooley moved between access points along the sublevel wall, opening one panel after another as he traced the path of the distribution grid. Each connection fed into the next with clean continuity, the system's design revealing itself piece by piece.

"Flow's consistent," he said. "No bottlenecks."

Milo, working from a nearby console, nodded without looking up. "Variance still within a tight band. It barely drifts."

Ashton stood near the central display, her attention not on the numbers themselves, but on the way they changed.

Or didn't.

Richard remained slightly apart from the others, watching the system as a whole rather than any single layer. From this distance, the movement resolved into patterns—smooth transitions, balanced adjustments, nothing abrupt.

Nothing unresolved.

Tomas observed with them, his posture relaxed but attentive.

"You'll find it holds," he said. "We've been running this configuration for years."

Dooley glanced back at him briefly.

"I believe you," he said. "That's not the question."

He reached for another panel, sliding it open with a quiet motion. Inside, the interface was older—less frequently used. The access point required a manual sequence before the display responded.

Dooley paused.

"That's interesting," he said.

"What is?" Milo asked.

"Override access," Dooley replied. "It's here—but not exactly available."

Tomas stepped closer, looking past him at the panel.

"It's restricted," he said. "We don't route through manual controls under normal operation."

"Normal operation isn't when you need them," Dooley said.

Tomas didn't respond immediately.

Instead, he reached past the panel and entered a short sequence. The system accepted it, but only after a brief delay.

"There are authorization layers," he said. "To prevent unnecessary intervention."

Dooley watched the delay.

"How long?" he asked.

"Under current conditions?" Tomas said. "Minimal."

"And under stress?" Dooley asked.

Tomas considered that for a moment.

"The system is designed to prevent stress conditions from escalating."

"That's not what I asked."

The exchange wasn't sharp.

Just precise.

Tomas met his gaze evenly.

"There would be a delay," he said.

Dooley nodded once, as if confirming something he already suspected.

"Thought so."

Across the room, Milo adjusted his display again, isolating a different section of the grid.

"I'm seeing the same thing here," he said. "Variance spikes are getting flattened before they propagate."

Ashton stepped closer, her eyes moving across the shifting data.

"It's not just flattening them," she said. "It's narrowing the range before they can form."

Milo glanced at her. "Preemptive?"

"Predictive," she said.

Tomas inclined his head slightly.

"That's correct."

He didn't sound defensive.

He sounded certain.

"It allows the system to remain stable without requiring intervention," he added.

Ashton's gaze remained on the display.

"It also means the system never experiences strain," she said.

Tomas didn't answer immediately.

He looked at the same data she was studying, then back at her.

"That's the goal," he said.

There was a brief silence.

Richard stepped closer to the central grid.

"And if strain does occur?" he asked.

Tomas turned slightly toward him.

"It hasn't," he said.

Richard held his gaze for a moment.

"That wasn't the question."

Again, there was no tension in the exchange.

Just clarity.

Tomas exhaled lightly.

"If it does," he said, "the system will respond."

Richard nodded once.

"And if the system can't?"

Tomas didn't answer right away.

The pause was small.

But it was there.

"Then we would," he said.

Dooley glanced again at the partially restricted panel.

"Eventually," he said.

Tomas didn't disagree.

The system continued its quiet operation around them, smoothing each fluctuation before it could fully form, keeping every measurable element within a narrow, controlled range.

From a distance, it looked flawless.

Up close, it was something else.

Not fragile.

But insulated.

Richard watched the flow of data as it moved across the central display, each adjustment feeding into the next with seamless continuity.

There was no visible strain.

No pressure building.

No moment where the system had to hold anything for long.

It resolved everything before it could become weight.

He didn't comment on it.

Instead, he turned slightly toward the others.

"Map every override point," he said. "Accessible or not."

Dooley nodded. "Already on it."

"Milo," Richard added, "track variance limits across all layers."

"Got it."

"Ashton—"

"I'm watching the pattern," she said.

Richard inclined his head once.

"Good."

They returned to their work.

Around them, the system held steady—absorbing, adjusting, smoothing.

Covering everything.

## Chapter 7 — Small Decisions

The transition out of the sublevels felt like stepping back into open air.

Not physically—the environment remained controlled—but the space widened, the ceilings lifted, and the steady hum of the deeper systems softened into the background of daily life.

Mira guided them through the upper corridor and out toward the habitat districts.

"The central systems handle most of the balancing," she said. "Out here you'll see how that translates."

The doors opened, and the plateau wind returned—soft, steady, moving across the open spaces between the structures.

The settlement stretched before them in quiet order.

Low buildings arranged with intention. Pathways clean and unobstructed. Small clusters of people moving through their routines without urgency.

Nothing felt rushed.

Nothing felt uncertain.

Mira walked at an easy pace, leading them along a path that curved gently between two residential clusters.

"This is Habitat B," she said. "Most of our population lives here."

Dooley glanced around, taking in the layout.

"Feels… calm," he said.

"It is," Mira replied.

They passed a small public space—a seating area bordered by low vegetation and a narrow water feature that reflected the sky above.

A man stood near the edge of the walkway, holding a small tablet. He paused, looking at the display for a moment, then adjusted his path slightly and continued on.

Not abruptly.

Just enough to align with something he had seen.

Milo slowed slightly as they passed.

"He changed direction," he said quietly.

Mira glanced back.

"Yes," she said. "Routing recommendation."

"Does that happen often?" Milo asked.

"Sometimes," she said. "It helps keep flow balanced."

They continued.

Further along, a woman stood near a distribution panel, selecting from a list of available items. She hesitated briefly, then tapped one option and nodded to herself as the panel confirmed the choice.

"Meal planning assistance," Mira said. "It helps reduce waste and maintain nutritional balance."

Dooley watched for a moment.

"She already knew what she wanted," he said.

Mira smiled slightly.

"It helps confirm it."

Ashton's gaze moved between the people and the panels, not focusing on any one interaction, but on the rhythm of them.

Pause.

Check.

Adjust.

Continue.

It wasn't forced.

It wasn't hesitant.

It was simply… how things were done.

Richard walked a few steps behind, taking in the movement of the settlement as a whole.

There was no tension in it.

No sign that anyone felt constrained.

If anything, there was a quiet ease to it—decisions made with confidence, supported by something trusted.

They turned toward a smaller path that led away from the central walkway.

"This way," Mira said. "You're meeting a local family."

---

The Maren home was modest but well-kept, its structure blending seamlessly with the surrounding habitat.

Jonah Maren met them at the entrance, his expression open and welcoming.

"You must be the cadets," he said. "We've been looking forward to this."

Lysa Maren joined him a moment later, greeting them with the same quiet warmth.

Inside, the space was simple—functional, comfortable, lived in.

A meal was already set, the table arranged with care but without formality.

"Please," Lysa said, gesturing. "Sit."

The conversation began easily.

Jonah spoke about his work in habitat maintenance, describing the routine checks and adjustments that kept their environment stable. Lysa talked about the agricultural dome, the way production cycles shifted with seasonal variations.

Nothing sounded complicated.

Everything sounded… managed.

"When the system recommends something," Jonah said at one point, "we know it's been modeled."

He offered a small shrug.

"That's reassuring."

Dooley nodded slightly.

"I can see that," he said.

There was no challenge in his voice.

Just acknowledgment.

Milo leaned forward slightly.

"Do you ever choose something different?" he asked.

Jonah considered that.

"Sometimes," he said. "But not often."

"Why not?" Milo asked.

Jonah glanced at Lysa, then back at Milo.

"It's usually right," he said.

There was no defensiveness in the answer.

Just experience.

Across the table, a younger voice spoke up.

"Why would you?"

Kira Maren sat quietly at first, watching the conversation with open curiosity. Now she leaned forward slightly, her attention fixed on Milo.

"Why would someone decide without checking first?" she asked.

The question wasn't challenging.

It wasn't skeptical.

It was simple.

Honest.

Milo hesitated—not because he didn't have an answer, but because he was deciding how to give it.

Before he could respond, Ashton spoke gently.

"Sometimes," she said, "you learn by trying."

Kira tilted her head slightly.

"But what if it's wrong?"

Ashton's expression didn't change.

"Then you learn something else," she said.

Kira considered that.

Jonah smiled faintly.

"We try not to be wrong," he said.

The room remained warm.

Comfortable.

No one felt corrected.

No one felt questioned.

The conversation shifted naturally after that—to Earth, to training, to the journey that had brought the cadets here.

But the question lingered.

Not in the room.

In the space between understanding and experience.

---

Later, as they stepped back outside, the wind moved gently across the plateau once more.

The settlement stretched around them, quiet and steady, each part moving in coordination with the rest.

Mira walked beside them, her tone light.

"That's a typical evening," she said. "Nothing unusual."

Dooley glanced back toward the Maren home.

"Feels like it," he said.

Milo walked a few steps behind, his attention distant for a moment.

"They don't feel controlled," he said quietly.

"No," Richard replied.

"They feel…" Milo searched for the word.

"Certain."

Ashton nodded slightly.

"They trust it," she said.

Richard looked out across the settlement again.

People moved through the pathways, pausing briefly at panels, adjusting, continuing.

No hesitation.

No resistance.

Just quiet alignment.

"Yes," he said.

"They do."

## Chapter 8 — The Edges of Control

The path curved outward from the habitat districts, gradually widening as the structures around them thinned.

Behind them, the settlement remained steady and complete—each building part of a working whole. Ahead, the plateau stretched more openly, the wind moving more freely across the grass.

Mira led without hesitation.

"This way," she said. "You've seen how we live. This is what comes next."

Dooley glanced ahead, narrowing his eyes slightly.

"Doesn't look like much," he said.

"It isn't," she replied. "Not yet."

As they walked farther from the central ring, the change became clearer.

The buildings here were spaced farther apart.

The pathways were marked, but less worn.

There were fewer people.

Then, beyond a low rise in the land, the expansion districts came into view.

They stood complete.

Not under construction. Not partially assembled.

Finished.

Structures arranged in the same careful pattern as the active habitats—residential clusters, support facilities, environmental nodes—all present and fully integrated into the surrounding layout.

But still.

No movement.

No activity.

No life.

Milo slowed as they approached.

"They're ready," he said.

"Yes," Mira replied.

"Fully?" Dooley asked.

She nodded.

"Structurally complete. Systems installed. Environmental controls in place."

"Powered?" he asked.

"Minimal," she said. "Baseline maintenance only."

They reached the outer edge of the first expansion district.

A wide access corridor led inward, ending at a sealed entry point set into the structure.

The door itself was smooth and unmarked except for a small interface panel beside it.

Inactive.

Dooley stepped closer, examining the panel.

"No wear," he said. "You haven't used this."

Mira shook her head.

"Not yet."

He glanced back at her.

"How long has it been ready?"

She hesitated.

"Several years," she said.

There was no discomfort in the answer.

Just a quiet awareness of it.

Milo moved past them, looking deeper into the district.

From this angle, the layout was easier to see—clean lines, organized clusters, everything positioned with the same deliberate care as the active habitats.

It wasn't abandoned.

It was waiting.

Ashton stepped forward, her gaze moving across the empty structures.

"It feels different," she said.

Mira looked at her.

"How?"

Ashton considered for a moment.

"The rest of the settlement feels… resolved," she said. "This doesn't."

Mira nodded slightly.

"That's fair."

She stepped closer to the access point, resting her hand lightly against the inactive panel.

"We built these after the system stabilized," she said. "Once we knew we could sustain growth."

"And you can't?" Milo asked.

"We can," she said.

There was a small pause.

"We've just been careful."

Dooley leaned back slightly, taking in the full district again.

"Careful about what?" he asked.

Mira didn't answer right away.

Instead, she looked out across the structures.

"Change," she said finally.

The word settled quietly between them.

Richard stepped forward, his attention moving not just across the district, but back toward the active settlement behind them.

"How much load increase?" he asked.

Mira turned slightly toward him.

"Full activation would increase environmental demand by just under thirty percent," she said. "Structural load adjustments would scale with population distribution."

Milo nodded, already processing it.

"That's manageable," he said.

"Yes," Mira replied.

"As long as the system can adapt," he added.

She inclined her head.

"It can."

Dooley glanced at the sealed entry again.

"But not like this," he said.

Mira didn't argue.

The wind moved across the open space between the structures, carrying with it the same steady rhythm as the rest of the plateau.

Nothing here was broken.

Nothing unfinished.

Just… unused.

Ashton stepped slightly farther into the corridor, stopping just short of the sealed door.

"It's not about whether it works," she said quietly.

Mira looked at her.

"No," she said. "It isn't."

Richard joined them at the edge of the district, his gaze moving once more between what was active… and what was not.

Behind them, the settlement continued its quiet, balanced operation.

Ahead, the expansion stood ready.

Waiting for something more than readiness.

Waiting for permission.

He didn't say it out loud.

But the thought settled clearly:

The system had made the colony stable.

It had also made it still.

## Chapter 9 — A Modest Act

---

The invitation came without ceremony.

Mira mentioned it as they walked back from the outer districts, her tone light, almost incidental.

"There's a small gathering this evening," she said. "We mark the founding cycle each year."

She glanced toward them briefly.

"It's nothing formal."

Dooley gave a faint smile.

"Those are usually the ones that matter," he said.

Mira didn't disagree.

---

The public plaza was quieter than Richard expected.

Not empty—but unhurried.

A small group had already gathered near the center, where the open space gave way to a gently curved path lined with low stone markers. Each one was set into the ground with deliberate spacing, forming a simple walkway that led toward the far edge of the plaza.

No banners.

No raised platform.

No amplification.

Just people.

Some stood in small groups, speaking softly. Others moved along the path at their own pace, pausing occasionally at one marker or another before continuing on.

The wind moved lightly across the plateau, brushing through the open space without interruption.

Mira slowed as they approached.

"This is the Founders' Walk," she said.

Her voice dropped slightly—not out of formality, but out of respect.

"The original settlement group is recorded here. We add to it each year."

Milo stepped closer to the first marker, his eyes scanning the simple inscription.

Names.

Dates.

Nothing more.

No titles.

No descriptions.

Just a quiet record of who had been there at the beginning.

Dooley moved alongside him, reading in silence.

"They kept it simple," he said.

"They wanted it that way," Mira replied. "They believed the work mattered more than the record of it."

Ashton walked a few steps ahead, her gaze moving slowly from one marker to the next.

Near the center of the path, one name appeared more frequently—referenced in small notations beside several entries.

Elijah Marron.

Not emphasized.

Just present.

Richard paused there, reading the name once, then again.

"Founder?" he asked quietly.

Mira nodded.

"One of the first," she said. "He helped organize the early structure—before the systems were in place."

Richard inclined his head slightly, then stepped forward again.

There was no formal start to the gathering.

No signal.

At some point, the conversations softened, and the small groups began to drift toward the center of the plaza, forming a loose circle around the opening of the walkway.

Elara Venn stood among them.

She wasn't elevated.

She didn't stand apart.

Just present, like the others.

After a moment, she spoke.

Her voice carried easily—not because it was raised, but because the space itself seemed to hold it.

"We mark another year," she said.

No introduction.

No ceremony.

Just the statement.

A few heads inclined slightly.

Someone near the edge of the group placed a small object at the base of the nearest marker—simple, unadorned. A token of some kind.

Elara continued.

"They built this place with what they had," she said. "And with what they didn't."

A faint ripple of recognition moved through the group.

"They learned quickly," she added.

A pause.

"They learned to be careful."

The words settled quietly.

No explanation followed.

None was needed.

Richard glanced briefly at the others.

Milo stood still, listening.

Ashton's gaze was lowered slightly, her attention fixed somewhere between the present and something just beyond it.

Dooley's posture had shifted—less relaxed now, more attentive.

Elara's voice softened.

"We remember them," she said. "Not for what went wrong… but for what they built after."

Another pause.

Then, simply:

"Thank you."

That was all.

No closing statement.

No instruction.

The gathering remained still for a moment longer, then began to move again—slowly, naturally, each person stepping forward in their own time to walk the path.

Mira gestured lightly.

"We usually walk," she said.

They followed.

The path curved gently, each marker placed just far enough apart to allow a pause without interrupting the flow.

Richard moved at a steady pace, his eyes passing over the names without trying to memorize them.

It wasn't about remembering each one.

It was about understanding that they had been there.

That they had built something that lasted.

Ahead of him, Milo stopped briefly at one marker, then continued on.

Dooley moved more slowly, reading each name in turn.

Ashton walked quietly, her steps measured, her attention somewhere deeper than the surface.

Near the end of the path, a small open space marked the final point of the walk.

No sign.

No designation.

Just a place where the markers stopped.

Mira stepped forward and placed her hand lightly against the last stone.

A simple gesture.

Nothing more.

Richard paused a few steps behind her.

The wind moved across the plateau again, carrying the same steady rhythm it always had.

For a moment, nothing else moved.

Then Mira stepped back.

"That's it," she said.

No one lingered longer than they needed to.

The gathering began to disperse—quietly, naturally, returning to the rhythms of the evening.

No closing announcement.

No formal end.

Just a continuation.

---

As they walked back toward the habitat district, Milo spoke first.

"They don't dwell on it," he said.

"No," Ashton replied.

"They remember," she added.

Dooley glanced back once toward the plaza.

"They built something solid," he said.

Richard didn't answer immediately.

He looked out across the settlement—the habitats, the pathways, the steady movement of people within a system that held everything in place.

"Yes," he said.

"They did."

## Chapter 10 — The Archive Room

---

The plaza had emptied without ever feeling full.

By the time they turned back toward the central complex, only a few people remained, moving quietly along the edges of the space or returning to their routines.

Mira walked beside them, her pace unhurried.

"There's one more place I'd like you to see," she said.

No one asked where.

They followed.

---

The Archive Room was not what Milo expected.

It was smaller than the rest of the complex—set slightly off from the main corridor, its entrance marked only by a narrow doorway and a simple panel.

No display.

No announcement.

Just a space that existed.

Mira stepped inside first, her voice lowering slightly—not out of formality, but instinct.

"This is where we keep the early records," she said.

The room was quiet.

Not empty—but still.

A single wall held a series of preserved items, each one set behind clear protective panels. Tools from the earliest construction phase. Handwritten logs. Small fragments of equipment that had long since been replaced by more advanced systems.

Nothing was arranged for effect.

Nothing highlighted.

Everything simply… there.

Richard stepped forward slowly, his attention drawn to a long, narrow ledger mounted near the center of the display.

The pages were preserved, but not hidden. The writing visible—precise, careful, written by hand.

Numbers filled most of the space.

Columns.

Allocations.

Dates.

At the bottom of one page, a series of signatures.

Steady lines.

Measured strokes.

He didn't read the details.

He didn't need to.

Behind him, the others moved quietly through the room.

Milo paused at one of the early system logs, his eyes tracing the transition from handwritten entries to printed records.

Dooley examined a set of older control levers—manual interfaces, worn slightly from use.

"They used to do everything directly," he said.

Mira nodded.

"They had to."

Ashton stood near the ledger, her gaze resting not on the numbers, but on the space between them.

On what they represented.

After a moment, Mira stepped back toward the doorway.

"I'll be outside," she said.

It wasn't an announcement.

Just a choice.

The cadets remained.

---

Elara Venn had entered without being noticed.

She stood near the far wall, her presence quiet, her attention fixed on the same ledger Richard had been studying.

She didn't speak.

She didn't move.

She simply remained.

Richard turned slightly, noticing her, then looked back at the ledger for a moment before speaking.

"You remember it," he said.

It wasn't a question.

Elara didn't look at him right away.

"Everyone does," she said.

Her voice was steady.

Measured.

After a brief pause, she stepped closer to the display.

"I remember standing on a crate," she said.

The words came simply.

No buildup.

"So I could reach the fountain."

Milo turned slightly toward her.

Elara's gaze remained on the ledger.

"They told us to drink slowly," she said. "So it would last."

A small pause.

"I didn't understand why."

Her hand rested lightly against the edge of the panel.

"People were quiet," she continued. "Quieter than usual."

Another pause.

"Not everyone woke up the next morning."

The room remained still.

No one interrupted.

No one asked for more.

Elara didn't offer it.

She looked down at the signatures at the bottom of the page.

"They made a decision," she said.

Her voice did not change.

"It made sense."

The words held.

Then:

"It still cost us."

Milo lowered his gaze slightly.

Dooley stood motionless near the control levers, his expression unreadable.

Ashton's eyes remained on the ledger, but her focus had shifted—no longer on the numbers, but on the weight behind them.

Elara exhaled quietly.

"We promised we would never guess again," she said.

She finally looked up, her eyes moving from the ledger to Richard.

"The system keeps that promise."

There was no defense in her voice.

No justification.

Just truth.

Richard met her gaze.

"And the cost?" he asked.

Elara considered that.

Then she shook her head slightly.

"It doesn't make that kind of mistake," she said.

The answer was clear.

But not complete.

No one pressed further.

After a moment, Elara stepped back from the display.

"That's why we're careful," she said.

She didn't wait for a response.

She turned and moved toward the doorway, leaving the room as quietly as she had entered.

---

The cadets remained for a moment longer.

No one spoke.

The room felt unchanged.

The same objects.

The same quiet.

But something had shifted.

Milo was the first to move.

"They learned from it," he said softly.

Ashton nodded once.

"Yes."

Milo hesitated, then added:

"But they stopped practicing."

The words settled.

Richard looked once more at the ledger—the numbers, the signatures, the steady lines drawn by people who had done what they believed was right.

Then he turned.

"Let's go," he said.

Outside, the plateau stretched wide beneath the fading light.

The settlement moved as it always had—quiet, balanced, certain.

Behind them, the Archive Room remained.

Unchanged.

Remembering.

## Chapter 11 — The First Adjustment

The Operations Complex felt different when they returned.

Nothing had changed.

The systems moved as they always had—steady, balanced, controlled. The same quiet precision filled the space, the same seamless coordination between every layer of the colony's infrastructure.

But now they understood it.

And that changed the way it felt.

Mira led them into the central chamber, where Tomas was already waiting near the primary console.

He looked up as they approached, his expression neutral but attentive.

"You've seen the Archive," he said.

It wasn't a question.

Richard nodded once.

"We have."

Tomas studied him for a moment, then glanced briefly at the others.

"Then you understand why we run the system the way we do."

"We understand why it matters," Richard said.

There was a difference.

Tomas seemed to register it.

He didn't challenge it.

Instead, he turned back toward the console.

"What are you proposing?" he asked.

Richard stepped forward slightly.

"A limited adjustment," he said. "Not activation."

Tomas waited.

"We widen the tolerance band in a controlled zone," Richard continued. "Small scale. Fully monitored."

"How small?" Tomas asked.

Milo brought up a section of the grid on a nearby display.

"Agricultural buffer region," he said. "North dome support layer. Low population impact."

Dooley added, "Minimal structural risk. Contained load shift."

Tomas studied the projection in silence.

"The system already maintains that region within optimal range," he said.

"Yes," Richard replied.

"And you want to move it outside that range."

"Slightly," Richard said.

Tomas exhaled slowly.

"For what purpose?"

Richard didn't answer immediately.

"To allow it to respond differently," he said.

Tomas looked at him.

"It already responds," he said.

"Before anything develops," Ashton said quietly.

The room settled again.

Tomas turned his attention back to the display, watching the steady flow of data across the agricultural support systems.

Nothing fluctuated.

Nothing strained.

Everything held.

"How long?" he asked.

"Short duration," Milo said. "Continuous monitoring. Immediate rollback available."

Dooley glanced toward the manual override panels along the wall.

"If needed," he added.

Tomas followed his glance.

That was enough.

After a moment, he nodded.

"Proceed," he said.

---

The preparation took time.

Not because the system resisted—but because the change required precision.

Dooley worked at the primary interface, isolating the selected region and mapping its current tolerance range. Milo tracked the live variance data, establishing baseline measurements. Ashton watched the system behavior as a whole, her attention fixed on the way the patterns formed and resolved.

Richard remained near the center, observing.

Tomas stood beside him.

"You're not increasing load," Tomas said.

"No," Richard replied.

"Just allowing variation."

"Yes."

Tomas considered that.

"It's a subtle distinction," he said.

Richard nodded.

"It is."

---

"Ready," Dooley said.

Milo confirmed. "Baseline stable."

Ashton didn't speak.

She was watching.

Richard gave a small nod.

"Go ahead."

---

The change was almost invisible.

On the display, a thin band widened—barely perceptible unless you knew exactly where to look.

The system registered the adjustment immediately.

For a moment, nothing happened.

Then—

A slight shift.

One of the environmental indicators moved just beyond its previous boundary.

Not far.

Not unstable.

Just… outside.

Milo leaned forward slightly.

"Variance increase detected," he said.

Dooley watched the response curve.

"It's not correcting," he said.

"It is," Ashton replied.

"Just not immediately."

The system adjusted.

But differently.

Instead of smoothing the fluctuation away instantly, it allowed it to persist—briefly—before guiding it back toward balance.

The motion was slower.

More natural.

Less forced.

Tomas watched the display closely.

"That's intentional?" he asked.

"Yes," Milo said. "We widened the acceptable range."

Tomas nodded once, though his expression remained focused.

Another fluctuation appeared—slightly larger this time.

Again, it remained visible for a moment before resolving.

No escalation.

No instability.

Just… movement.

Richard's gaze shifted from the display to the larger system map.

The change was localized.

Contained.

But real.

---

Above them, the colony continued.

In the agricultural dome, minor adjustments passed through the environmental systems—temperature gradients shifting slightly, moisture levels redistributing with less immediate correction.

Nothing noticeable to the eye.

Nothing disruptive.

Just a subtle difference in how the system moved.

---

Back in the control chamber, Dooley stepped back slightly.

"Still within safe margins," he said.

Milo nodded. "No cascading effects."

Ashton's voice came softly.

"It's breathing," she said.

Tomas glanced at her.

She didn't explain.

She didn't need to.

Richard watched the system for a moment longer.

There was no strain.

No instability.

But there was something new.

A small space where variation could exist—if only briefly.

"Maintain for another cycle," he said.

Dooley nodded.

---

After a few minutes, Milo spoke again.

"All readings stable," he said.

Tomas exhaled slowly.

No tension left his shoulders.

Just… a quiet release.

"It holds," he said.

Richard inclined his head.

"Yes."

Tomas looked at the display once more, then back at Richard.

"It's a small change," he said.

"Yes."

Tomas considered that.

Then:

"It matters."

Richard didn't respond.

He didn't need to.

---

As the system continued its adjusted rhythm, the colony above moved as it always had—steady, certain, unchanged in appearance.

But beneath it, something had shifted.
Not enough to be seen.
Not enough to be felt.
But enough to exist.

## Chapter 12 — What the System Doesn't See

---

The adjustment held.

That was the first thing they confirmed.

By the time the next cycle completed, the agricultural buffer region had remained within its expanded tolerance range without any sign of instability. The system adapted to the change without resistance, integrating the wider variance into its balancing patterns as though it had always been there.

On the surface, nothing had changed.

But the data told a slightly different story.

Milo stood at the central console, layering two sets of projections over one another.

"Baseline predictive model," he said, indicating the first set. "And adjusted model under expanded tolerance."

The displays overlapped—lines tracing nearly identical paths across the grid.

Nearly.

Dooley leaned in slightly.

"That's a difference," he said.

"Small," Milo replied. "But consistent."

Tomas stepped closer, his attention narrowing.

"What kind of difference?" he asked.

Milo isolated a segment of the data, magnifying the comparison.

"The system predicted immediate correction," he said. "But with the wider tolerance, it allowed the fluctuation to persist before resolving."

"That was intentional," Tomas said.

"Yes," Milo replied. "But the model didn't adjust immediately. It assumed the original behavior."

Tomas watched the display for a moment.

"Then it updated," he said.

"It did," Milo agreed.

After the fact.

The distinction remained unspoken.

---

Ashton stood slightly apart, her gaze moving between the layers of data.

"It expects patterns," she said quietly.

Milo nodded.

"That's how it predicts," he said.

Ashton tilted her head slightly.

"But it expects them to continue."

Tomas glanced toward her.

"That's the basis of any predictive model," he said.

"Yes," she said.

Her tone remained even.

"But people don't always continue."

The room settled around that.

Not as a contradiction.

Just an addition.

---

Mira, who had been observing quietly from the edge of the chamber, stepped forward slightly.

"There are times when someone chooses differently," she said.

The others turned toward her.

"Not often," she added. "But it happens."

Dooley gave a small nod.

"Give me an example."

Mira considered for a moment.

"Routing," she said. "The system might recommend a path to balance movement across the habitat. Most people follow it."

"Most," Dooley said.

"Yes," Mira replied. "But sometimes someone doesn't."

"What happens then?" Milo asked.

"The system adjusts," she said. "It compensates."

"How quickly?" Dooley asked.

Mira hesitated.

"Not as quickly," she said.

---

Milo brought up a routing simulation, overlaying predicted movement patterns with recorded deviations.

"There," he said, pointing to a small divergence in the data. "User deviation from recommended path."

The system compensated.

But not immediately.

For a brief interval, the flow became uneven.

Nothing disruptive.

Nothing unstable.

Just… imperfect.

Ashton watched the pattern.

"It corrects after the choice," she said.

"Yes," Milo replied.

"It doesn't anticipate the choice itself."

"No," he said.

---

Tomas folded his arms, his gaze steady on the display.

"It can't," he said.

There was no defensiveness in the statement.

Just clarity.

Milo nodded.

"It models behavior," he said. "Not intent."

Richard stepped closer, his attention moving from the localized data to the system as a whole.

"And when behavior changes?" he asked.

Tomas answered without hesitation.

"It adapts."

Richard inclined his head slightly.

After.

The word wasn't spoken.

But it remained.

---

Another data set came into view—this time from the agricultural dome.

A minor delay in response time.

A small variation in environmental balance.

Again, nothing significant.

Nothing that would be noticed without looking for it.

But present.

Dooley tapped the display lightly.

"You built it to assume cooperation," he said.

Tomas considered that.

"We built it to assume consistency," he said.

Dooley gave a faint smile.

"Same thing," he said.

Mira shook her head slightly.

"Not always," she said.

The group glanced toward her.

"Sometimes consistency changes," she added.

---

The system continued its work around them—balancing, adjusting, responding within its expanded range.

It still held.

It still worked.

But now, the edges were visible.

Not as flaws.

As boundaries.

Richard watched the shifting patterns for a moment longer.

"The system does what it's designed to do," he said.

Tomas nodded.

"Yes."

Richard's gaze remained steady.

"It just doesn't do everything."

The words settled quietly.

Tomas didn't respond immediately.

He didn't argue.

He simply watched the data.

For a long moment.

---

Milo adjusted the display again, narrowing the focus back to the adjusted region.

"All systems stable," he said.

"Within expanded tolerance," Dooley added.

Ashton didn't speak.

She was still watching the pattern.

Richard stepped back slightly.

"Continue monitoring," he said.

---

The system carried on.

Balancing.

Responding.

Adapting.

But now, just beneath the surface, something else was visible.

Not instability.

Not failure.

Just the space where a decision had not yet been made.

## Chapter 13 — Pressure Without Warning

The system settled into its adjusted rhythm.

Time passed in quiet continuity—measured in cycles, not moments. The widened tolerance remained active, the agricultural buffer continuing to operate within its expanded range without visible disruption.

The displays reflected stability.

But not stillness.

Subtle movement persisted—fluctuations forming and resolving with a slightly slower cadence than before.

Ashton watched it without speaking.

Milo tracked it in numbers.

Dooley leaned back against the console, arms loosely folded.

Tomas stood beside them, his attention steady.

Nothing pressed.

Nothing strained.

Until—

Milo's display shifted.

Not dramatically.

Just enough to draw his focus.

"Hold," he said quietly.

Dooley straightened.

"What is it?"

Milo isolated the region.

"Agricultural dome north," he said. "Humidity spike."

Tomas glanced at the central display.

"That's within range," he said.

"Yes," Milo replied.

"But rising."

---

On the larger grid, a small section brightened—subtle, but distinct.

The system responded immediately.

Ventilation adjusted.

Temperature gradients shifted.

Moisture redistribution initiated.

For a moment, it appeared to resolve.

Then—

The humidity dropped slightly below baseline.

Dooley leaned in.

"Overcorrection," he said.

The system compensated again.

Humidity rose.

Not to the original level.

Higher.

Milo's brow furrowed.

"It's oscillating," he said.

Ashton stepped closer, her eyes fixed on the pattern.

"Not randomly," she said. "It's chasing the balance point."

The system adjusted again.

Lower.

Then higher.

Each movement smaller than the last—but still present.

Tomas watched closely.

"It will settle," he said.

No one disagreed.

But no one looked away.

---

"Variance increasing within tolerance," Milo said.

Dooley's eyes tracked the response curve.

"It's not smoothing it out," he said.

"No," Ashton replied.

"It can't."

The word wasn't emphasized.

It didn't need to be.

---

The system continued its adjustments.

Each correction closer to center.

Each oscillation smaller.

But not gone.

Richard stepped forward slightly, his attention shifting between the localized event and the system as a whole.

"Any propagation?" he asked.

Milo checked the surrounding regions.

"None," he said. "Contained."

"Structural impact?" Richard asked.

"Negligible," Dooley replied.

Tomas nodded once.

"Then we let it resolve."

---

Seconds passed.

Then minutes.

The oscillation persisted—diminishing, but present.

The system was working.

But it was working differently.

More… visibly.

Ashton's voice came softly.

"It's holding the adjustment," she said.

Not eliminating it.

Holding it.

---

Another cycle passed.

The fluctuation narrowed again.

Closer.

Closer.

Then—

Still.

Milo exhaled lightly.

"Stabilized," he said.

Dooley straightened, stepping back from the console.

"Clean resolution," he said.

Tomas nodded.

"Yes."

But his gaze remained on the display a moment longer.

---

The system resumed its quiet balance.

The agricultural dome returned to steady environmental control.

No alarms had sounded.

No intervention had been required.

Everything remained within safe margins.

And yet—

Dooley tapped the console lightly.

"That took longer than it should have," he said.

Tomas didn't respond immediately.

"No," he said after a moment.

"It took exactly as long as it needed to."

Dooley gave a faint, thoughtful smile.

"That's one way to say it."

---

Milo brought up the recorded sequence, replaying the oscillation curve.

"Without the expanded tolerance," he said, "it would have been flattened immediately."

"Yes," Tomas said.

"And now?" Milo asked.

Tomas looked at the data.

"Now it resolves differently."

---

Ashton stepped back slightly, her gaze moving across the system as a whole.

"It had to carry it," she said.

The others turned toward her.

"The fluctuation," she added. "It didn't remove it. It held it until it could settle."

Richard nodded once.

"And it did."

---

The room grew quiet again.

Not with tension.

With awareness.

Tomas folded his arms, his posture unchanged—but his attention deeper now.

"It remained stable," he said.

"Yes," Richard replied.

Tomas nodded.

"That matters."

Richard met his gaze.

"It does."

A brief pause.

Then:

"So does how it got there."

---

The system continued.

Balanced.

Responsive.

But no longer invisible in its corrections.

Now, when pressure appeared—

It had to handle it.

## Chapter 14 — The Question of Control

---

The system returned to its steady rhythm.

The oscillation event passed into the record—logged, analyzed, resolved. The agricultural dome continued its operation without interruption, the widened tolerance still active, the system adapting to its new parameters with quiet consistency.

Nothing remained of the fluctuation.

Except the memory of how it had moved.

Dooley replayed the sequence once more, watching the curve narrow and settle.

"Still clean," he said.

Milo nodded. "No residual drift."

Ashton didn't look at the display.

She didn't need to.

Richard stood slightly apart, his attention no longer fixed on the event itself, but on the space it had created.

Tomas remained near the central console.

He hadn't moved.

---

After a moment, he spoke.

"Under the original parameters," he said, "that would have resolved instantly."

No one disagreed.

"Yes," Milo said.

Tomas kept his gaze on the display.

"No oscillation," he continued. "No visible variance."

"Correct," Milo said.

Tomas nodded once.

"And now?"

He didn't finish the thought.

He didn't need to.

Dooley answered.

"Now it resolves… honestly," he said.

Tomas glanced toward him.

"That's one way to put it."

Dooley gave a small shrug.

"It had to carry the imbalance," he said. "Couldn't just erase it."

Tomas looked back at the display.

"It wasn't erased before," he said.

"It was," Ashton said quietly.

The room stilled slightly.

Tomas turned toward her.

She met his gaze.

"Not the condition," she said. "The appearance of it."

A small distinction.

But not a small difference.

Tomas considered that.

---

He shifted his attention to the manual override panels along the far wall.

"We would not have intervened before," he said.

"No," Richard replied.

"The system would have handled it."

"Yes."

Tomas folded his arms.

"And now?"

The question settled into the room.

Not directed.

Just present.

Dooley glanced at the override panels.

"Now you have the option," he said.

Tomas looked at him.

"We always had the option."

Dooley didn't disagree.

"You had access," he said. "That's not the same thing."

---

Milo brought up the response timeline from the oscillation event.

"From initial spike to full stabilization," he said, "we're looking at a longer window than baseline."

Tomas nodded.

"Yes."

Milo hesitated slightly.

"If conditions escalated faster than the system could compensate…"

He didn't finish.

Tomas did.

"There would be a gap."

The word settled quietly.

---

Richard stepped forward, his gaze steady.

"The system is designed to prevent that," Tomas said.

"Yes," Richard replied.

"And it has."

"Yes."

Tomas exhaled slowly.

"But if it doesn't?"

Again, no one rushed to answer.

Not because they didn't know.

Because the answer mattered.

---

Ashton spoke first.

"Then someone has to decide," she said.

The words were simple.

Not heavy.

But they held.

Tomas looked at her.

"That's what we moved away from," he said.

"Yes," she replied.

Her tone remained even.

"And that's what remains."

---

The room grew quiet again.

Not tense.

Not uncertain.

Just still.

Mira, standing near the edge of the chamber, watched without speaking. Her expression had changed—not dramatically, but enough to show that she was listening differently now.

Dooley shifted his weight slightly, glancing once more at the override panels.

"They haven't been used in years," he said.

Tomas nodded.

"That's correct."

Dooley's gaze remained on them.

"That doesn't mean they shouldn't work."

Tomas didn't respond.

He didn't need to.

---

Milo adjusted the display again, bringing up a broader system view.

"All systems stable," he said.

The words were familiar now.

Expected.

But they carried something more than reassurance.

They carried context.

---

Richard looked at Tomas.

"You built something that holds," he said.

Tomas met his gaze.

"Yes."

Richard nodded once.

"And now you're deciding what happens when it doesn't have to."

Tomas considered that.

It wasn't a correction.

It wasn't a challenge.

Just a statement placed where it could be seen.

---

For a long moment, no one spoke.

The system continued its quiet operation around them—balancing, adjusting, maintaining the steady state it had been designed to protect.

Tomas watched it.

Not as something to rely on.

But as something to understand.

Finally, he spoke.

"If the system cannot act immediately…"

He paused.

The words were measured.

Carefully placed.

"…then someone must."

No one responded.

No one needed to.

---

The system continued.

Steady.

Reliable.

And now—

Observed.

## Chapter 15 — Certification

---

Preparation took less time than expected.

Not because the work was simple—but because the conclusions were clear.

Milo finalized the data sets, aligning baseline projections with the adjusted system behavior. Dooley reviewed the structural response logs, confirming stability across all monitored regions. Ashton moved quietly between the displays, not checking numbers, but confirming that the patterns held.

Richard watched the system as a whole.

It remained steady.

Not unchanged.

But steady.

Tomas stood beside them, his attention no longer divided between trust and observation.

Now, he simply watched.

---

The Council chamber was smaller than Richard expected.

A single table.

Six seats.

No elevated positions.

No display walls beyond a central projection panel embedded into the surface.

Functional.

Deliberate.

Elara Venn was already there when they entered, seated among the others.

She looked up as they approached, her expression calm, attentive.

Not guarded.

Not expectant.

Just present.

"Thank you for coming," she said.

Richard inclined his head slightly.

"Thank you for receiving us."

The others took their places without formality.

No one announced the beginning.

No one needed to.

---

Milo activated the central display.

The system map appeared—clean, structured, familiar.

He began with the baseline.

"Current system stability remains within established parameters," he said. "No structural deviations. No environmental imbalance."

The Council listened.

No interruptions.

No reactions beyond quiet attention.

He shifted to the adjusted model.

"We implemented a controlled expansion of tolerance in the agricultural buffer region," he continued. "Variance increased within safe margins. No cascading effects observed."

Dooley added, "Structural response remained stable throughout."

Milo nodded.

"As expected."

He brought up the oscillation event.

"A localized fluctuation occurred during the test window," he said. "The system responded within expanded tolerance."

The curve appeared—visible now, no longer smoothed away.

"It resolved without intervention," Milo said.

He paused.

"But not immediately."

That distinction remained.

---

Elara leaned slightly forward.

"Was it contained?" she asked.

"Yes," Milo replied. "No propagation beyond the initial region."

"And if it had not been?" another council member asked.

Milo glanced briefly at Richard.

Then answered.

"Manual intervention would have been required."

The room remained quiet.

---

Tomas spoke for the first time.

"Override access points are available," he said. "Though not currently optimized for rapid response."

A few council members exchanged brief glances.

Not concern.

Awareness.

---

Elara's gaze returned to the display.

"The system remains stable," she said.

"Yes," Richard replied.

"And Phase Two?"

Richard held her gaze.

"Technically viable," he said.

No embellishment.

No assurance beyond that.

---

Elara considered the projection in silence for a moment.

Then:

"How much error are we allowing?"

The question settled into the room.

Not sharp.

Not fearful.

Just precise.

---

Richard didn't answer immediately.

He stepped slightly closer to the table, his attention on the system map as it continued its quiet motion.

"We're not introducing error," he said.

A small pause.

"We're allowing variation."

Elara watched him.

"And the difference?" she asked.

Richard met her gaze.

"The system still corrects," he said. "It just doesn't remove every fluctuation before it exists."

Elara leaned back slightly.

"That means we see it."

"Yes."

"And respond to it."

"Yes."

---

Another council member spoke.

"And if the response is wrong?"

The question was simple.

Direct.

Richard didn't avoid it.

"Then it can be corrected," he said.

No elaboration.

No reassurance beyond that.

---

The room remained still.

Not uncertain.

Just thoughtful.

---

Elara looked down briefly at the display, then back at the group.

"You're telling us the system holds," she said.

"Yes," Richard replied.

"And that it requires awareness."

"Yes."

"And, at times, decision."

Richard nodded once.

"Yes."

---

Tomas spoke again, his voice steady.

"If the system cannot act immediately," he said, "someone must."

Elara turned slightly toward him.

She didn't question it.

She acknowledged it.

---

A long moment passed.

No one rushed it.

No one filled the silence.

Finally, Elara inclined her head slightly.

"The system is ready," she said.

It wasn't an announcement.

It was a conclusion.

A few of the other council members nodded in agreement.

"Certification is granted," she continued.

The words settled quietly.

---

No one reacted outwardly.

There was no shift in posture.

No visible relief.

Just a shared understanding.

---

Elara's voice softened slightly.

"Activation," she said, "will require further consideration."

Richard inclined his head.

"Of course."

---

The display dimmed.

The meeting concluded as simply as it had begun.

No formal closing.

No dismissal.

Just a natural end.

---

As they stepped out of the chamber, the corridor beyond felt unchanged.

The system continued.

The settlement remained steady.

Nothing had shifted.

And yet—

Everything had moved forward.

---

Milo spoke quietly as they walked.

"They agreed," he said.

"Yes," Richard replied.

Dooley glanced back once toward the chamber.

"That wasn't the hard part," he said.

Ashton nodded slightly.

"No," she said.

---

Richard looked ahead, his gaze steady.

"No," he said.

"It wasn't."

## Chapter 16 — The Decision to Proceed

---

The corridor outside the Council chamber was quiet.

The cadets stepped away without discussion, their work complete for the moment, their role shifting from action to waiting.

Behind them, the door closed.

No announcement.

No signal.

Just a separation.

---

Inside, the room remained unchanged.

The display dimmed.

The table still.

The system map no longer active.

Only the Council remained.

---

For a time, no one spoke.

Not because there was nothing to say.

Because what needed to be said required space.

---

Elara Venn rested her hands lightly on the table.

Her gaze remained steady—not on any one person, but on the space before her.

"They've shown us the system holds," she said.

A few quiet nods followed.

"That was never the only question," another member replied.

"No," Elara said.

"It wasn't."

---

Tomas Hale stood near the far side of the table.

Not seated.

Not removed.

Present.

"The system performs within expanded tolerance," he said. "It remains stable."

No one challenged that.

"And?" one of the members asked.

Tomas considered the question.

"It requires awareness," he said.

A pause.

"And response."

---

The words settled.

Not heavily.

But clearly.

---

Another council member leaned forward slightly.

"We built this system so we wouldn't have to make those decisions," they said.

Elara nodded once.

"Yes."

"And now we're being asked to take them back."

Elara didn't answer immediately.

---

She looked down at the table for a moment, her expression unchanged.

Then:

"We never gave them away," she said.

The room stilled slightly.

"We deferred them," she continued. "Because we had to."

A quiet breath.

"Because we made a choice once… and it cost us."

No one needed clarification.

No one asked for it.

---

Tomas spoke again, his voice even.

"The system still protects us," he said.

Elara looked toward him.

"Yes," she said.

"But not completely."

Tomas held her gaze.

"No," he said.

---

The silence that followed was different.

Not uncertain.

Not hesitant.

Just… honest.

---

A council member near the far side of the table spoke.

"If we proceed," they said, "we accept that there will be moments where the system does not decide for us."

"Yes," Elara said.

"And we accept responsibility for those moments."

"Yes."

---

Another voice, quieter.

"And if we are wrong?"

Elara didn't look away.

"Then we will correct it," she said.

The answer came without emphasis.

Without reassurance beyond itself.

---

Tomas shifted slightly, his posture unchanged, but his presence more defined now.

"If the system cannot act immediately," he said, "someone must."

Elara inclined her head.

"We understand that."

---

The room settled again.

No one spoke.

No one needed to.

The question had already been asked.

Not in words.

In understanding.

---

Elara looked around the table.

Not seeking agreement.

Recognizing it.

---

"We built this place to last," she said.

A small pause.

"Not to remain the same."

The words rested there.

Simple.

Clear.

---

She drew a quiet breath.

"Phase Two activation is authorized," she said.

---

No one reacted outwardly.

No one needed to.

The decision had not been sudden.

It had been forming long before this moment.

---

After a moment, one of the council members nodded.

Then another.

Tomas remained still for a moment longer.

Then inclined his head once.

---

The meeting ended as it had begun.

Without ceremony.

Without declaration.

Just a natural conclusion to what had already been decided.

---

The door opened.

---

The cadets looked up as Elara stepped into the corridor.

Her expression had not changed.

But something in her presence had.

Not lighter.

Not heavier.

Just… settled.

---

"It's approved," she said.

No elaboration.

No formality.

---

Richard nodded once.

"Understood."

---

Dooley glanced briefly at the others.

"That was quick," he said.

Milo shook his head slightly.

"No," he said.

"It wasn't."

---

Ashton looked toward Elara for a moment, then back toward the central complex.

"They've been deciding that for a long time," she said.

---

Elara met her gaze briefly.

"Yes," she said.

---

Richard turned slightly toward the operations wing.

"Let's prepare," he said.

---

The system continued.

Steady.

Reliable.

Unchanged.

---

But now—

It would be asked to do something more.

## Chapter 17 — Activation

---

The Operations & Safety Complex felt different.

Not in its structure.

Not in its systems.

But in its stillness.

Everyone was present.

The cadets stood near the central console, each positioned where they had worked throughout the previous cycles. Tomas remained at the primary interface. Mira stood just behind the outer ring, her attention moving between the displays and the people gathered around them.

The Council had taken their places without formality.

No elevated positions.

No separation.

Just a shared presence within the space where the system lived.

Elara Venn stood nearest the central control panel.

Her posture was steady.

Unchanged.

---

Milo reviewed the final system state.

"All regions stable," he said. "Baseline within operational limits."

Dooley checked the structural grid.

"Load distribution holding," he added.

Ashton didn't speak.

She was watching the pattern.

Richard looked once across the room—not at the system, but at the people.

Then he nodded.

"We're ready."

---

Tomas turned slightly toward Elara.

No words were exchanged.

None were needed.

---

Elara stepped forward.

Her hand rested lightly on the activation interface.

For a moment, she did not move.

Not hesitation.

Recognition.

Then—

She initiated the sequence.

---

There was no visible surge.

No audible shift.

No dramatic change.

The system accepted the command.

---

On the central display, the tolerance bands expanded.

Not suddenly.

Not sharply.

Gradually.

Across the network, each region adjusted in sequence—agricultural systems, habitat zones, structural supports, environmental controls—all widening their acceptable ranges, allowing more variation to exist within the system.

The flow changed.

Subtly.

But completely.

---

Milo watched the data.

"Expansion confirmed," he said.

Dooley tracked the load transitions.

"No instability," he added.

Tomas remained focused on the central grid.

"System adapting," he said.

---

The colony above continued as it always had.

No alarms.

No visible disruption.

Just movement.

---

Then—

Milo's display shifted.

"Hold," he said quietly.

---

A small divergence appeared in the routing grid within Habitat B.

Two movement streams intersecting.

Not large.

Not disruptive.

But enough to create imbalance.

---

The system responded.

It presented options.
It calculated adjustments.
It displayed projected outcomes.

---

And then—
It stopped.

---

Dooley leaned slightly forward.
"It's not resolving it," he said.
Milo nodded.
"It's waiting."

---

The display held.
Options remained visible.
Predictions updated.
But no action was taken.

---

Ashton spoke softly.
"It's asking."

---

No one moved immediately.
No one rushed to respond.
The moment was not urgent.
But it was real.

---

Elara stepped closer to the display.
Her eyes moved across the options.
Projected flow adjustments.
Resource reallocations.
Timing variations.

Each one valid.

Each one incomplete.

---

The room remained still.

Not tense.

Not uncertain.

Just… waiting.

---

Richard did not speak.

He did not guide.

He did not explain.

---

Elara considered the projections.

Then reached forward.

---

She selected one.

---

The system responded immediately.

The routing adjusted.

The imbalance resolved.

The flow continued.

---

No delay.

No hesitation.

Just… integration.

---

Milo exhaled softly.

"Stabilized," he said.

---

Dooley leaned back slightly.

"That was it," he said.

---

Tomas remained still for a moment longer.

Then nodded once.

"Yes."

---

Ashton watched the system for another moment.

"It didn't fail," she said.

"No," Richard replied.

"It didn't need to."

---

Elara stepped back from the console.

Her expression had not changed.

But something in her posture had settled.

Not relief.

Not pride.

Just… acceptance.

---

Around them, the system continued.

Balanced.

Responsive.

But now—

Not alone.

---

Mira let out a quiet breath she hadn't realized she was holding.

"That's new," she said.

---

Richard looked at the central display once more.

The system moved as it always had.

But now, within it—

There was space.

---

He turned slightly toward the others.

“It holds,” he said.

---

No one disagreed.

## Chapter 18 — The Horizon Holds

---

Morning came without announcement.

The plateau stretched beneath the same wide sky, the wind moving across the grass with its familiar, steady rhythm. From a distance, the settlement appeared unchanged—structures in place, pathways clear, systems operating with the same quiet precision they always had.

Nothing had shifted.

And yet—

---

The central plaza carried a slightly different pace.

People moved as they had before—calm, deliberate, unhurried. Some paused at the public panels, reviewing recommendations, confirming routes or selections before continuing on.

Others did not.

A man stepped past a routing display without stopping, adjusting his direction slightly on his own before merging into the flow.

A woman paused at a resource panel, considered the recommendation… then chose differently.

No disruption followed.

No correction pressed down immediately.

The system adjusted.

And continued.

---

Milo noticed it first.

"They're not all checking," he said quietly.

Dooley followed his gaze.

"They still can," he said.

"Yes," Milo replied.

"They just don't always."

---

Mira walked beside them, her expression thoughtful.

"It feels the same," she said.

Ashton shook her head slightly.

"It isn't," she said.

---

They turned toward the Maren home.

Jonah greeted them with the same steady warmth as before, though his posture held a subtle difference—less reliance, more awareness.

Inside, the morning routine moved easily.

Lysa prepared the meal.

Kira sat at the table, a small panel open in front of her.

She studied it for a moment.

Then closed it.

Milo noticed.

"You didn't check," he said.

Kira looked up at him.

"I did earlier," she said.

A small pause.

"I wanted to try it this way."

Milo nodded once.

"And?"

Kira gave a small shrug.

"I'll see."

---

No one corrected her.

No one intervened.

The moment passed as naturally as any other.

---

Later, in the Operations Complex, the system moved as it always had—balanced, responsive, steady.

But the room felt different.

Not quieter.

Not louder.

More… present.

Tomas stood at the central console, his attention moving between the displays and the team around him.

He didn't stand apart from the system anymore.

He stood with it.

---

Dooley checked one of the manual override panels, running a quick diagnostic.

"Access is faster," he said.

Tomas nodded.

"It needed to be."

No elaboration.

No justification.

Just a statement.

---

Milo brought up the system-wide map.

"All regions stable," he said.

The words were familiar.

But now they meant something more.

---

Richard looked across the chamber, then toward the outer districts beyond.

"Expansion status?" he asked.

Mira smiled slightly.

"Partial activation," she said.

---

They walked back toward the edge of the settlement.

This time, the expansion district was not still.

The access doors stood open.

Not fully.

Just enough.

Inside, movement had begun.

A small number of people walked through the newly active spaces, their pace measured, their attention aware—not hesitant, but not automatic either.

The district no longer felt like something waiting.

It felt like something beginning.

---

Ashton paused at the threshold.

"They stepped into it," she said.

Richard nodded.

"Yes."

---

Elara Venn approached quietly, her presence as steady as it had always been.

She looked out across the district, then back toward the settlement behind them.

"It holds," she said.

Richard met her gaze.

"Yes."

A brief pause.

Then she added:

"So do we."

---

No one responded.

No one needed to.

---

The transport stood ready at the edge of the plateau.

The cadets made their way toward it without urgency, their work complete, their presence no longer required.

Mira walked with them part of the way, then stopped.

"Thank you," she said.

Dooley gave a small nod.

"You did the hard part," he said.

Mira shook her head slightly.

"We're just starting," she said.

---

Milo looked back once more toward the settlement.

"They'll be fine," he said.

Ashton's gaze followed his.

"They'll learn," she said.

---

Richard paused before boarding, his attention resting for a moment on the horizon beyond the plateau.

Wide.

Open.

Unfinished.

---

Behind them, the system continued.

Steady.

Reliable.

But no longer alone in its work.

---

He stepped aboard.

---

The transport lifted smoothly, rising above the plateau as the settlement spread out below—ordered, balanced, alive.

Not unchanged.

Not unstable.

Just… moving forward.

---

The horizon held.

## Epilogue — After the First Decision

---

The plateau felt the same in the evening.

The wind moved across the grass in long, steady lines. The settlement stood in its familiar pattern—structures set with intention, pathways clean, systems operating with quiet precision beneath it all.

From a distance, nothing had changed.

---

Inside the Operations & Safety Complex, the lights had dimmed to their night cycle.

The central chamber was no longer full.

Most had returned to their routines, the cadence of the day settling back into its usual rhythm. A smaller team remained—monitoring, observing, adjusting where needed.

Tomas Hale stood near the primary console.

Not alone.

Not apart.

Just present.

---

The system moved across the display in its steady flow—data shifting, balancing, resolving.

He watched it without urgency.

Without assumption.

---

A small indicator shifted near the edge of the grid.

Not a warning.

Not even an alert.

Just a change.

A routing imbalance in one of the newly active expansion corridors.

Two movement paths intersecting again.

Similar to before.

But not identical.

---

The system responded.

It presented options.

Projected adjustments.

Calculated outcomes.

---

And then—

It waited.

---

Tomas didn't call for assistance.

He didn't step away.

He didn't hesitate.

He simply watched.

---

The projections updated slightly as new data came in—timing variations, density adjustments, alternative routing paths.

Each one viable.

Each one incomplete.

---

For a moment, he did nothing.

Not because he didn't know what to do.

Because he understood what it meant to choose.

---

A technician nearby glanced toward him.

"Do you want me to route it?" she asked.

Tomas shook his head slightly.

"No," he said.

His voice was calm.

Measured.

"I'll take this one."

---

He stepped forward.

---

His hand hovered briefly over the interface.

Not uncertain.

Just aware.

---

Then he made the selection.

---

The system responded immediately.

The flow adjusted.

The imbalance resolved.

The movement continued.

---

No delay.

No correction needed after.

Just integration.

---

The technician nodded once, already returning her attention to her own station.

"Clean," she said.

---

Tomas remained at the console for a moment longer.

The system continued.

Balanced.

Responsive.

Still doing what it had always done.

---

But now—

Not doing it alone.

---

He stepped back.

Not far.

Just enough to see the whole.

---

Across the display, small variations appeared and resolved—some automatically, some presented, some simply allowed to pass within the wider range.

Nothing out of control.

Nothing demanding.

Just movement.

---

Mira entered quietly from the side corridor.

She paused near the edge of the chamber, watching the system for a moment before stepping closer.

"How is it?" she asked.

Tomas didn't look away from the display.

"It holds," he said.

Mira smiled slightly.

"That's what you said yesterday."

---

Tomas nodded once.

"Yes."

A brief pause.

Then:

"It's different."

---

Mira followed his gaze across the system map.

In one corner, a minor fluctuation appeared—held briefly, then resolved without intervention.

She watched it happen.

"It doesn't feel as tight," she said.

"No," Tomas replied.

"It isn't."

---

Another small decision point appeared.

The system presented it.

Waited.

Then adjusted based on input from another station across the room.

---

Mira tilted her head slightly.

"We're part of it now," she said.

---

Tomas allowed a faint, almost imperceptible smile.

"We always were," he said.

A small pause.

"We just weren't practicing."

---

Mira nodded slowly.

---

They stood there for a while, watching the system move.

Not for problems.

Not for failure.

Just… watching.

---

Outside, the plateau stretched wide beneath the evening sky.

The settlement moved in quiet continuity—people walking, choosing, pausing, continuing.

Not perfectly.

Not unpredictably.

Just… naturally.

---

Inside, the system held.

---

And so did they.

## Cadet Log — Richard Hale

---

**Cadet Log — Richard Hale**

**UESC Specter One**

**Post-Mission Entry**

---

We completed certification.

Phase Two is active.

The system is holding.

---

From a technical standpoint, the mission was successful.

Structural load distribution remained within expected tolerances. Environmental systems adapted without instability. Manual overrides integrated cleanly.

There were no failures.

No emergency corrections.

No cascading events.

---

That will be the official record.

---

But that's not what I'll remember.

---

What I'll remember is how long it took for anyone to make a decision once the system paused.

---

Not because they didn't understand the situation.

Not because they weren't capable.

Because they had learned not to.

---

It wasn't hesitation the way we usually think of it.

It was something quieter.

A kind of restraint.

---

They had built something that protected them.

And over time, they trusted it completely.

---

It worked.

It still works.

---

That's what made this assignment different.

We weren't sent to fix something that was broken.

We were sent to verify something that had worked for a long time.

---

And then… to widen it.

---

Widening tolerance sounds simple when you say it that way.

In practice, it means allowing variation.

Allowing uncertainty.

Allowing outcomes that aren't fully predicted.

---

For a system, that's a calibration.

For people, it's something else.

---

I don't think they were afraid of failure.

Not exactly.

---

They remembered it.

---

We saw part of that in the Archive Room.

Not the event itself.

Just the record of it.

Numbers written down.

Names beside them.

A decision that made sense at the time.

And still cost something.

---

They built their system so they would never have to make that kind of decision again.

---

And it worked so well… they stopped practicing.

---

Milo said something during the mission.

He didn't realize how much it stayed with me.

---

"They learned from the mistake," he said.

Ashton answered him.

"Yes."

Then he said,

"But they stopped practicing."

---

That was the moment I understood what Phase Two really required.

---

It wasn't just a system upgrade.

It was a return.

---

Not to the same conditions.

Not to the same risks.

But to the responsibility of choosing when outcomes aren't guaranteed.

---

We didn't teach them that.

We didn't tell them to do it.

---

We just created a space where it was necessary again.

---

The first time the system paused, the room felt different.

Not unstable.

Just… open.

---

No one moved right away.

---

Then someone did.

---

It was a small decision.

Routine, by most standards.

But it mattered.

Because it wasn't assigned.

It wasn't calculated all the way through.

It was chosen.

---

And nothing failed.

---

I think that's what they needed to see.

Not that the system could handle more.

But that they could.

---

There's a tendency to think responsibility is something you either have or don't have.

I don't think that's true anymore.

---

I think it's something you can step away from.

Quietly.

Gradually.

Until one day you realize you haven't carried it in a long time.

---

And stepping back into it… feels heavier than it should.

---

They didn't step all the way back in.

Not yet.

---

But they shifted.

---

That's enough for now.

---

We left the settlement this morning.

From orbit, everything looked the same.

Same layout.

Same structure.

Same balance.

---

But I don't think it is.

---

The system is still there.
Still doing what it was built to do.

---

The difference is smaller than it sounds.
And larger than it looks.

---

They're part of it again.

---

End Log.

## Cadet Reference Manual

**Phase One**

The original settlement operating model based on strict predictive optimization.

All major systems—power, environment, structural load, and resource allocation—are managed through centralized modeling designed to minimize risk and prevent instability.

Human decisions are supported, but over time became largely replaced by system-directed outcomes.

---

**Phase Two**

An upgraded operational framework that expands system tolerance ranges.

Instead of tightly smoothing all variation, Phase Two allows controlled fluctuations and requires selective human input during certain decision points.

Purpose:

- Increase adaptability
- Support expansion
- Reintroduce human participation in system management

---

**Optimization Engine**

The central system located within the Operations & Safety Complex.

It continuously monitors and adjusts:

- environmental conditions
- power distribution
- structural load balancing
- resource allocation

Designed to prevent instability by predicting and smoothing potential imbalances before they occur.

---

**Founding Stability Protocol**

A system-wide operational philosophy developed after an early settlement crisis.

Core principles:

- rely on predictive modeling
- minimize human estimation during critical decisions
- prevent resource misallocation
- prioritize long-term stability

Over time, this protocol became deeply integrated into both system behavior and cultural practice.

---

**Tolerance Range**

The acceptable level of variation within system operations.

In Phase One:

- very narrow
- fluctuations minimized

In Phase Two:

- widened deliberately
- allows natural variation and human decision points

---

**Manual Override System**

A set of physical and software-based controls that allow human operators to intervene directly in system operations.

Originally installed during early settlement phases, but rarely used once full optimization was established.

Reintroduced and updated during Phase Two certification.

---

**Structural Load Balancing**

The process of distributing physical and operational stress across the settlement's infrastructure.

Includes:

- habitat pressure management
- dome support distribution
- expansion readiness
- environmental compensation

Maintained automatically by the Optimization Engine, with human oversight during Phase Two.

---

**Operations & Safety Complex**

The central hub of the settlement.

Functions include:

- system monitoring
- environmental control
- structural management
- emergency coordination

Houses the Optimization Engine and primary control interfaces.

---

**Expansion Districts**

Pre-constructed but inactive settlement zones located beyond the primary habitat ring.

Activated during Phase Two to:

- increase population capacity
- expand operational range
- introduce additional system load

Serve as the primary driver for Phase Two implementation.

**Archive Room**

A quiet space near the Operations & Safety Complex that preserves early settlement records.

Contains:

- original system logs
- resource allocation records
- early tools and documentation
- the founding drought ledger

Serves as a place of remembrance and a reminder of the settlement's early challenges.

---

**Founding Incident (Drought Allocation Failure)**

An early settlement crisis during Phase One in which water resources were redistributed during a drought.

The decision:

- preserved agricultural output
- delayed supply to a residential sector
- resulted in the loss of two colonists

This event led directly to the development of the Founding Stability Protocol.

---

**System Smoothing**

A process by which the Optimization Engine automatically adjusts variables to prevent visible fluctuations.

Results in:

- stable outcomes
- minimal disruption
- reduced need for human decision-making

In Phase Two, smoothing is reduced to allow controlled variation.

**Transit Hub / Public Plaza**

A central gathering space used for:

- arrivals and departures
- public announcements
- remembrance events
- community gatherings

Serves as both a functional and symbolic center of the settlement.

## Historical Appendix — When Navigation Became Certain

---

For most of human history, navigating the open ocean required constant judgment.

Sailors could not rely on a single instrument or system. Instead, they used a combination of observation, experience, and interpretation:

- The position of the stars
- The angle of the sun
- The movement of waves
- The direction of wind
- The feel of the vessel beneath them

Navigation was not a single calculation.

It was a continuous process of decision-making under uncertainty.

---

**What Skilled Navigators Did**

A skilled navigator did more than follow a route.

They constantly adjusted:

- correcting for drift
- estimating position between known points
- responding to changing weather
- choosing when to alter course

Every decision carried consequence.

Every correction required judgment.

---

This work could not be automated.

It had to be practiced.

---

**The Arrival of Precision Systems**

In the modern era, navigation changed.

With the development of satellite-based positioning systems such as GPS, location could be determined with extraordinary accuracy.

Ships could:

- identify their exact position instantly
- follow pre-programmed routes
- maintain course automatically
- reduce the need for continuous human estimation

From a safety and efficiency standpoint, the improvement was undeniable.

Navigation became easier.

More reliable.

Less dependent on individual interpretation.

---

The system worked.

---

**What Quietly Changed**

As these systems became standard, the role of the navigator began to shift.

Instead of constantly interpreting conditions, crews increasingly:

- monitored instruments
- confirmed system outputs
- followed established digital routes

The ocean had not changed.

But how people engaged with it had.

---

The skill of navigation was still taught.
But it was used less often.

---

Over time, a subtle shift occurred:
The practice of decision-making under uncertainty became less familiar.

---

**When Systems Were Not Enough**

In situations where electronic navigation systems failed—or provided incorrect data—crews were required to return to manual navigation.
Investigations into several maritime incidents revealed a pattern:
The knowledge was still present.
But the habit of using it was not.

---

Crews hesitated.
Not because they did not understand what to do—
But because they had not been doing it regularly.

---

The system had reduced error.
But it had also reduced practice.

---

**What Changed in Response**

Modern maritime training did not reject navigation systems.
Instead, it adapted.
Crews are now required to:

- practice manual navigation techniques
- verify system outputs independently
- maintain awareness beyond automated displays
- remain actively engaged in decision-making

The goal became balance.

---

Systems would guide.
But people would remain responsible.

---

**Why This Matters**

Reliable systems do more than solve problems.
They change behavior.

---

When outcomes become predictable, the need to decide appears to decrease.
When the need to decide decreases, the habit of deciding begins to fade.

---

This does not happen suddenly.
It happens quietly.
Through success.

---

The danger is not that people forget how to choose.
It is that they stop needing to.

---

And when the moment returns that requires it—
The weight of that choice feels unfamiliar.

---

**The Enduring Principle**

Modern navigation did not return to uncertainty.
It returned to participation.

---

The systems remained.
The knowledge remained.

---

But the responsibility was reclaimed.

---

Because no matter how precise a system becomes—
Direction still belongs to the one who chooses it.

## About the Series — Living in the Delta Era

---

**Living in the Delta Era**

The Delta Era is no longer theoretical.

It has become a way of operating.

What once felt like preparation has settled into practice. The cadets now serve in a reality where certainty is rare, clarity often arrives too late to guide decisions, and success cannot always be measured by what was fixed, prevented, or publicly explained.

Systems still function.

Procedures still matter.

But experience has taught them that not every outcome should be controlled—and not every problem should be solved for others.

---

In this phase of the series, growth is no longer measured by visible results.

It is measured by discernment.

---

The cadets are learning not only when to act—but when to step back. They are discovering that responsibility is not something to be taken by default, even when they have the ability to carry it. Some of the most important moments now require them to restore responsibility to others—and trust them to bear it.

This is not inaction.

It is restraint.

---

The Delta Era explores a deeper truth:

That faithfulness is not always rewarded with understanding,

and responsibility does not always arrive with permission.

And now, something more:

That responsibility, once surrendered, must be relearned—
and cannot be carried on someone else's behalf.

---

These stories continue to value courage, loyalty, and friendship—but they place them under quieter pressures.
Trust must coexist with caution.
Authority must be exercised without certainty.
And leadership must sometimes choose not to solve—so that others can learn to choose.

---

The missions grow more complex not because the universe is louder—
but because it has learned how to remain silent.

---

The 7-Second Signal marked the threshold.
The stories that followed confirmed the change.
This book continues that path.

---

Here, the cadets are not sent to repair failure.
They are sent to verify strength—and in doing so, they uncover something quieter:
That a system can remain stable,
while the people within it step away from decision.
And that restoring balance may require less control, not more.

---

From this point forward, the Delta Era continues to deepen.
Listening matters as much as action.
Restraint matters as much as intervention.
And some of the most meaningful victories may come when

responsibility is returned—
not retained.

---

The Delta Era is not about what is revealed.
It is about what is recognized—
and responsibly left in the right hands.

## Author's Note

---

This story is not about failure.

It is about people who learned from a real loss—and built something that worked.

Their system protected them.

It reduced risk.

It prevented the kind of mistake that had once cost them dearly.

And for a long time, that was enough.

---

The cadets were not sent to fix what they found.

They were sent to verify it.

And in doing so, they encountered something quieter than a problem:

A people who had learned to be careful—

and had slowly stopped practicing what it means to choose.

---

There is a difference between avoiding mistakes

and avoiding responsibility.

At first, that difference can be difficult to see.

Both can look like stability.

Both can produce good outcomes.

But over time, one builds strength—

and the other quietly replaces it.

---

Responsibility is not only about making the right decision.

It is about being willing to make one when outcomes are not guaranteed.

That willingness is not automatic.

It must be practiced.

---

The colony in this story did not refuse responsibility.

They protected themselves from it.

And in doing so, they lost the habit of carrying it.

---

This story does not suggest that systems are wrong.

They are necessary.

They protect, stabilize, and support.

But they cannot replace the act of choosing.

---

At some point, responsibility must return to the individual.

Not all at once.

Not perfectly.

But deliberately.

---

The most important moment in this story is not a success.

It is a decision.

A small one.

Made without certainty.

Carried without guarantee.

---

That is where growth begins again.

---

Thank you for reading.

## About the Author

Russell McFall is the creator of the *Space Cadet Legacy* series, a long-running collection of clean, character-driven science fiction written for readers of all ages.

A lifelong storyteller, Russell's earliest tales began as bedtime adventures for his children—stories shaped by curiosity, humor, and a steady conviction that courage, friendship, and integrity matter just as much as technology and exploration. Over time, those stories grew into a shared universe that continues to expand while remaining grounded in moral clarity and hope.

Russell brings a distinctive blend of life experience to his writing. With a background in software development, many years in children's ministry, and a deep commitment to faith-based values, his stories emphasize thoughtful decision-making, personal responsibility, and restraint. Conflict is real, consequences are honest, and solutions favor wisdom over force—without preaching or cynicism.

The Delta Era of *Space Cadet Legacy* reflects a natural progression—both in the characters and in the author's vision. As the cadets mature, the challenges they face grow quieter and more complex. Listening matters as much as action. Responsibility must sometimes be returned, not carried. And integrity must hold even when outcomes are uncertain and recognition does not follow.

Russell continues to write with a simple goal:

to tell stories that entertain, encourage, and remind readers—young and old alike—that even in a vast and uncertain universe, character still counts.

When he isn't writing, Russell enjoys reflecting on history, faith, and the unseen moments that shape lives—quiet decisions and uncelebrated acts of integrity that often matter far more than they appear.

## Also by Russell McFall

*Ordained Path Books*

Clean Science Fiction and Inspirational Writing for Thoughtful Readers

---

### Contemporary Fiction and Short Stories

Stories of Community, Memory, and Hope

- **Squirrel Creek Estates — Where the Porch Lights Stay On**
- **The World That Chose**

---

### The Space Cadet Richard Series

*Where the Legacy Began*

- **The Final Countdown**
- **The Dunes of Dinkytown**
- **The Mastermind's Maze**

---

### The Space Cadet Legacy Series

*Over 30+ novels of courage, friendship, and discovery — including*

- **The First Gate**
- **Welcome Back, Player**
- **Flibber's Journey Home**
- **Stronger Together**
- **Phasegate Rising**
- **The Makers' Handshake**

*(New missions continuing.)*

**Literary Humor and Reflections**

**Serious Nonsense — Sanity Sold Separately**

**Devotional and Reflection Books**

- **Remembering God's Help — Stone by Stone**
- **Attributes of God**
- **This Is My Story, This Is My Song**
- **Lives of Faith**
- **Foundations of Faith**

Russell McFall writes clean fiction and thoughtful reflections designed to uplift the heart, sharpen the mind, and remind every reader that light still wins.

www.ingramcontent.com/pod-product-compliance
Lightning Source LLC
LaVergne TN
LVHW010948110826
845149LV00015B/3258